HIPPOS GO BERSERK!

WRITTEN AND ILLUSTRATED BY SANDRA BOYNTON

Aladdin Paperbacks

"*I* didn't invite them. Did *you* invite them?"
(For Mom and Dad, with love.)

Simon & Schuster Books for Young Readers
An imprint of Simon & Schuster Children's Publishing Division
1230 Avenue of the Americas
New York, NY 10020

Also available in a Simon & Schuster Books for Young Readers
hardcover edition.

The text of this book was set in Times Roman.

Manufactured in China 0917 SCP
20 19 18 17 16 15 14 13 12

Library of Congress Catalog Card Number: 96-84706

ISBN 978-0-689-80818-0

One hippo, all alone,

calls two hippos

on the phone.

3

Three hippos at the door

4

bring along another four.

Five hippos come overdressed.

Six hippos show up with a guest.

Seven hippos

arrive in a sack.

8

Eight hippos
sneak in the back.

Nine hippos

come to work.

ALL THE HIPPOS

GO BERSERK!

All through the hippo night,
    hippos play with great delight.

But at the hippo break of day,
the hippos all must go away.

9

Nine hippos and a beast join

eight hippos riding east, while

seven hippos moving west leave

six hippos quite distressed, and

5 five hippos then set forth with

four hippos headed north.

Three hippos say, "Good day."

The last two hippos go their way.

One hippo, alone once more,

misses the other forty-four.